sleep

MEG AND
CATHERINE PYBUS

Snorey time

It's time to go to sleep

ILLUSTRATED BY
PETRA BROWN

templar publishing

To Keith, the original Snorey – C.P. & M.P.
For Patricia – P.B.

This book belongs to
a little Snorey called
. . . .

A TEMPLAR BOOK

First published in the UK in 2012 by Templar Publishing
This softback edition published in 2013 by Templar Publishing,
an imprint of The Templar Company Limited,
Deepdene Lodge, Deepdene Avenue, Dorking, Surrey, RH5 4AT, UK
www.templarco.co.uk

Text copyright © 2012 by Catherine Pybus and Meg Pybus
Illustration copyright © 2012 by Petra Brown
Design copyright © 2012 by The Templar Company Limited

1 3 5 7 9 10 8 6 4 2

ISBN 978-1-84877-944-0

Designed by Mike Jolley

Printed in China

Down on Dozy Down
the dormice love to sleep,

especially the Snoreys.

Daddy Snorey is fast asleep.

Mummy Snorey is fast asleep.

Snuggle, Snuffle, Pillow and Mop
are fast asleep.

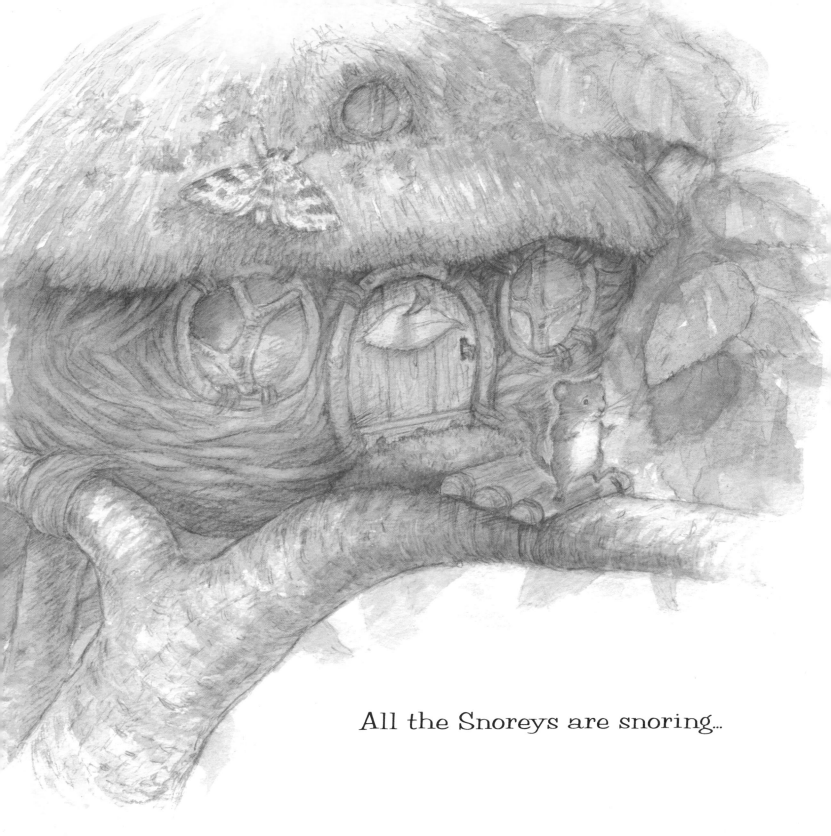

All the Snoreys are snoring...

all except Pignut.

"All good little Dormice are fast asleep,"
said Batty the Bat, hanging from a branch.

"I'm not at all sleepy," said Pignut.

"Come up here and hang from your feet,"
yawned Batty, "you'll soon drop off!"

"Whoopsie!"

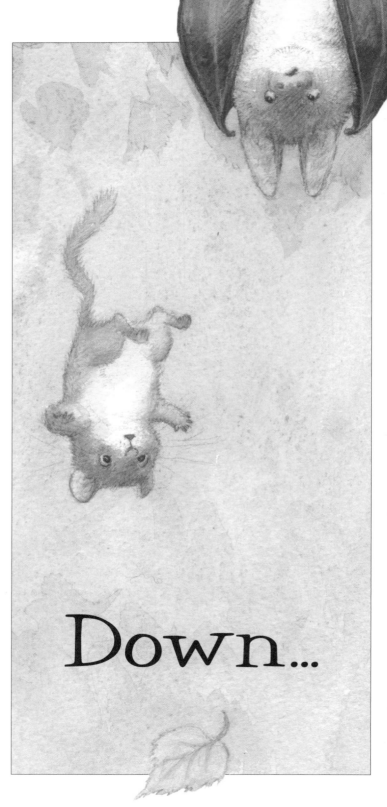

Down...

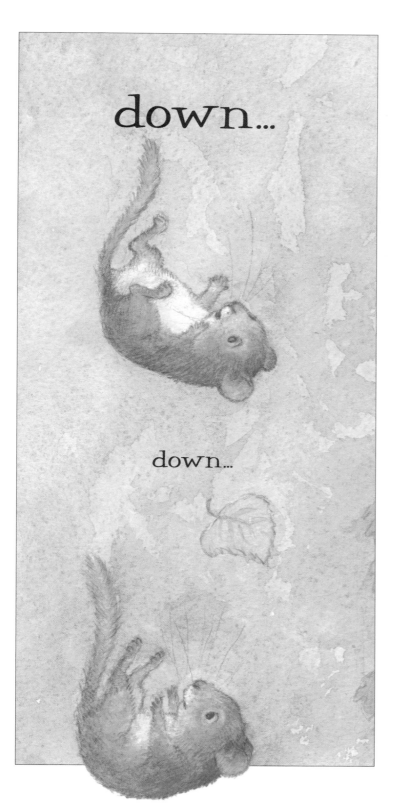

down...

down...

Pignut landed
with a scrunch
in a pile of leaves.

"Ouch!" said the pile of leaves.

"Ouch!" said Pignut.

"All good little Dormice are fast asleep,"
said Hodge the half-asleep Hedgehog.

"I'm not at all sleepy," yawned Pignut.

"Curl into a ball and roll in leaves,"
rustled Hodge. "You'll soon feel tired."

So Pignut curled up and rolled...

and rolled...

and rolled.

Down... down...

down...

Plop!

...straight into Dozy Down Pond.

Pignut climbed onto a lily pad.

And slowly the lily pad began
to drift… and drift… and drift.

Round, and round, and round Dozy Down pond.

"I'm not at all sleepy," said Pignut,
"but I'll just have a little nap."

So Pignut settled down for a doze.
"All good little Dormice are fast asleep,"
croaked Splodge the Toad from under the lily pad.

And in one enormous leap,
Splodge sploshed out of Dozy Down Pond
with Pignut still on his head.

Down...

down...

down.

Pignut landed safe and soft
in Mummy Snorey's arms.

"All good
little dormice are
fast asleep," said Mummy.

"But I'm not at all sleepy,"
said Pignut.

"Do you know how dormice go to sleep?"
asked Mummy.

Pignut shook her head.

"It's time for The Secret Book of Sleep,"
said Mummy.

Pignut cuddled next to Snuggle, Snuffle,
Pillow and Mop.

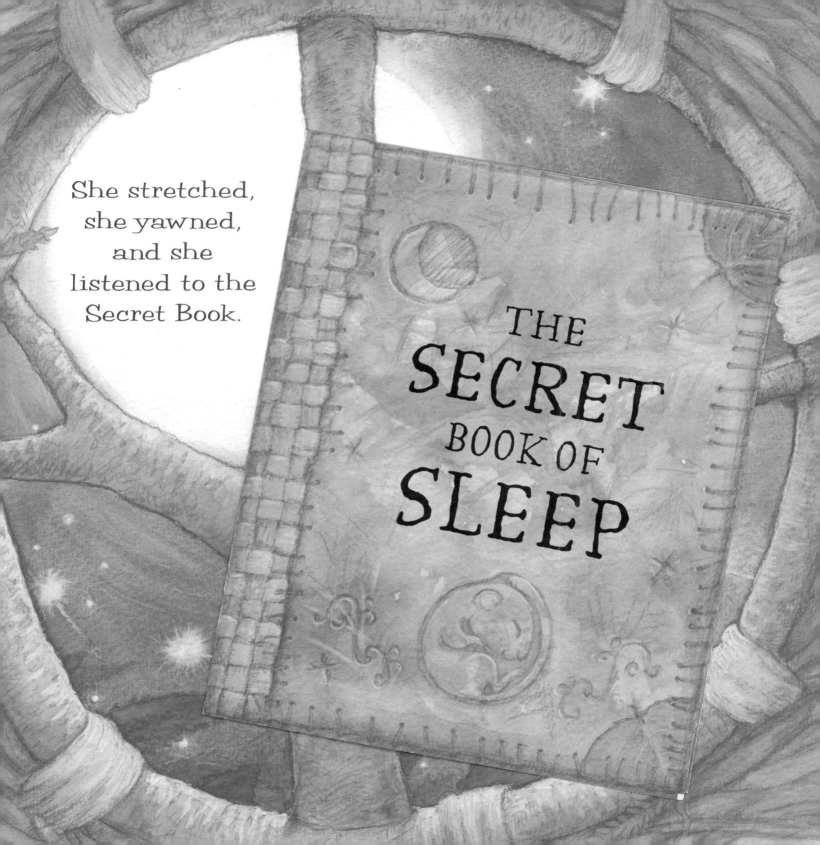

She stretched,
she yawned,
and she
listened to the
Secret Book.

THE
SECRET
BOOK OF
SLEEP

"I'm not at all…"

but Pignut was already
in a deep and dreamy Snorey sleep.